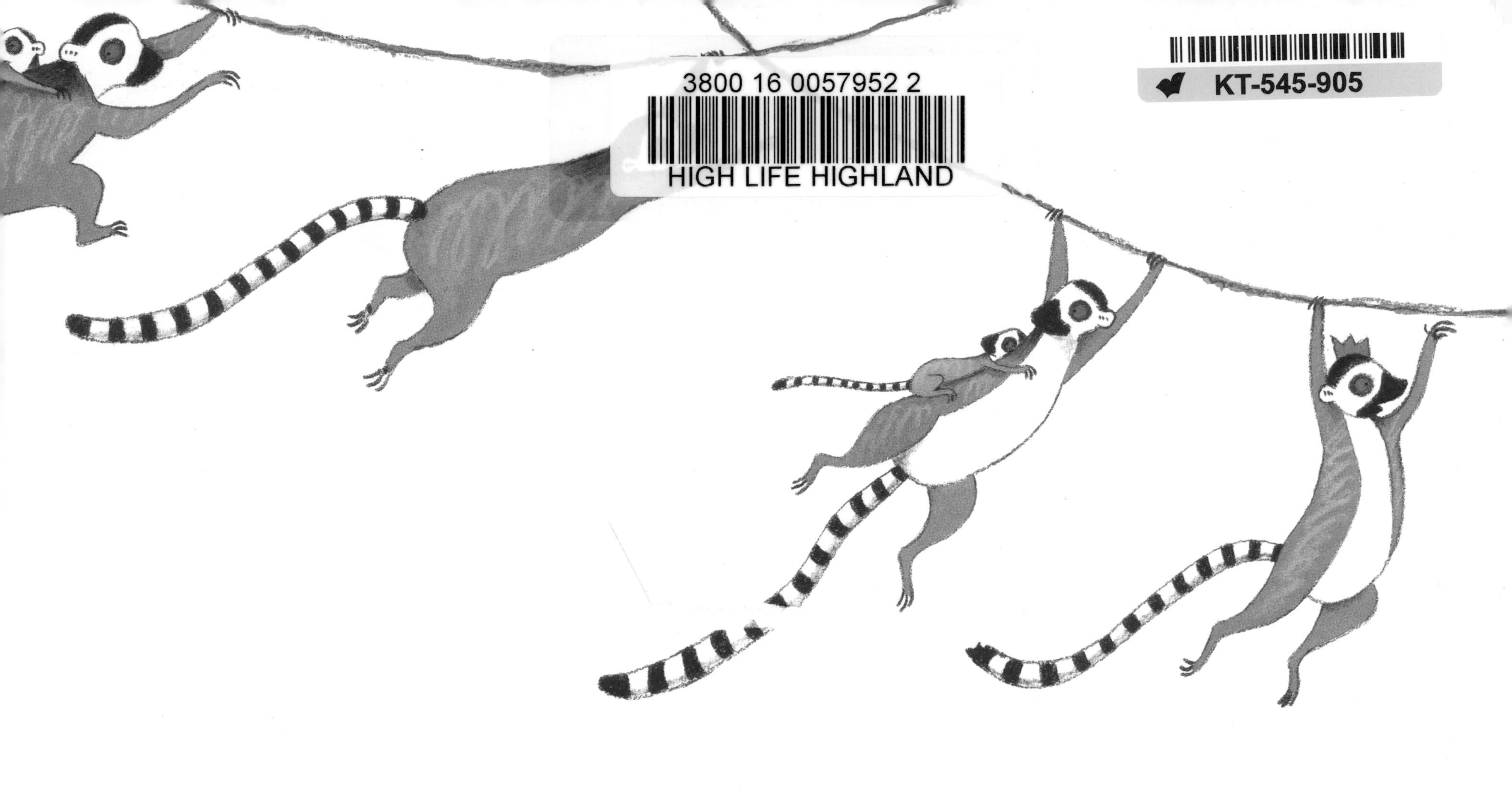

This book belongs to:

....

For Karen

First published in 2015 by
Hodder Children's Books
This paperback edition published in 2016

Hodder Children's Books
An imprint of Hachette Children's Group
Part of Hodder & Stoughton
Carmelite House
50 Victoria Embankment
London EC4Y 0DZ

A catalogue record of this book is available
from the British Library.

ISBN: 978 1 444 91946 2
10 9 8 7 6 5 4 3 2 1

Printed in China

An Hachette UK Company

www.hachette.co.uk

MIX
Paper from
responsible sources
FSC® C104740
FSC
www.fsc.org

Ellie Sandall

Follow Me!

It's time to wake up!
Come down from the tree.

Follow me,
follow me,
follow me!

Places to be,

things to do, things to see.

Follow me, follow me, follow me!

Things to hunt,
things to chase,

things to race.
things to scare,
Follow me,
follow me,
follow me!

Things to climb,
things to meet,

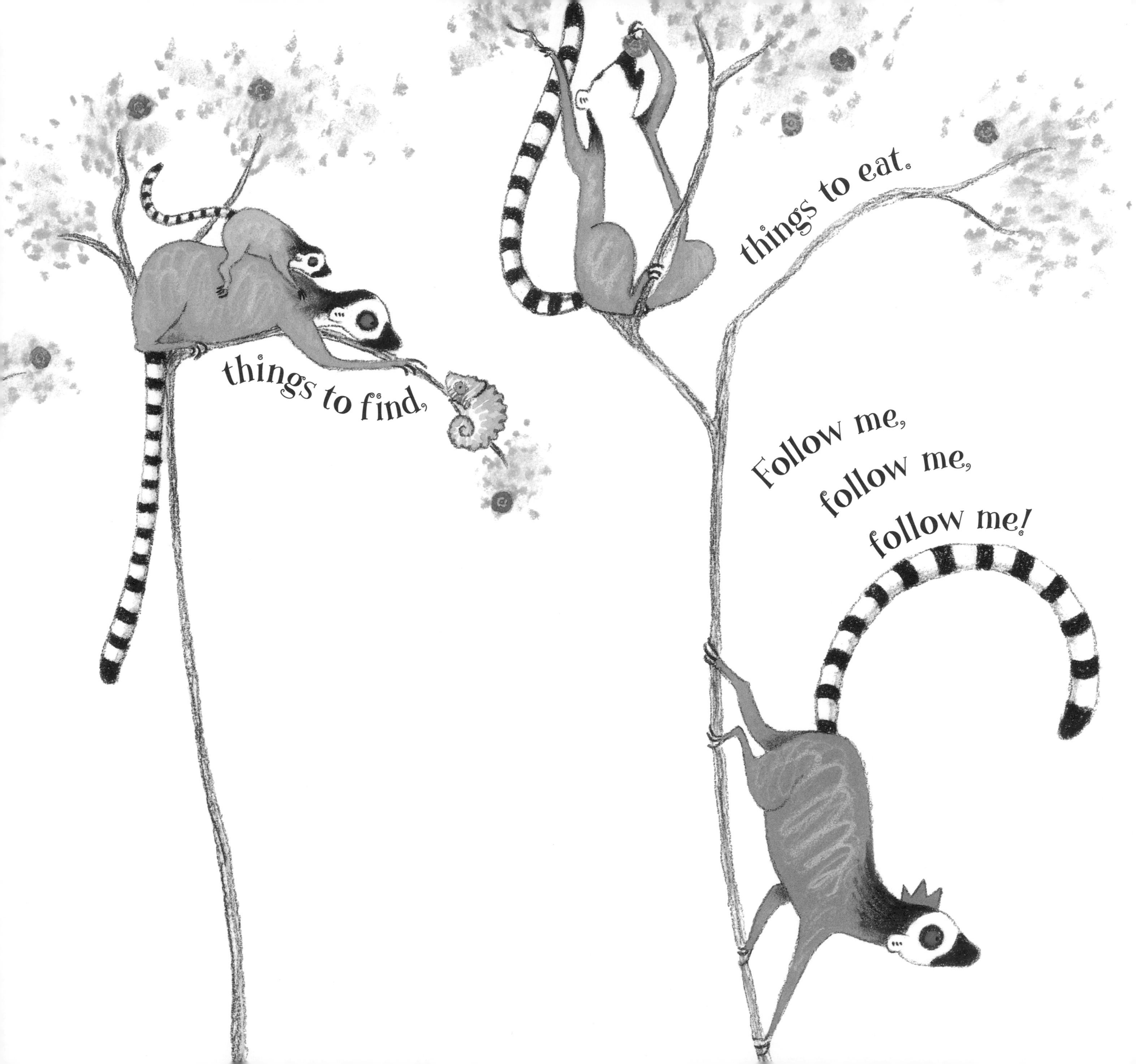
things to find,
things to eat.
Follow me,
follow me,
follow me!

Things to chew,

things to munch,

things to have
for our lunch.

Follow me,
follow me,
follow me!

Things to jump,
things to hop,
things to leap,
things to...

STOP!

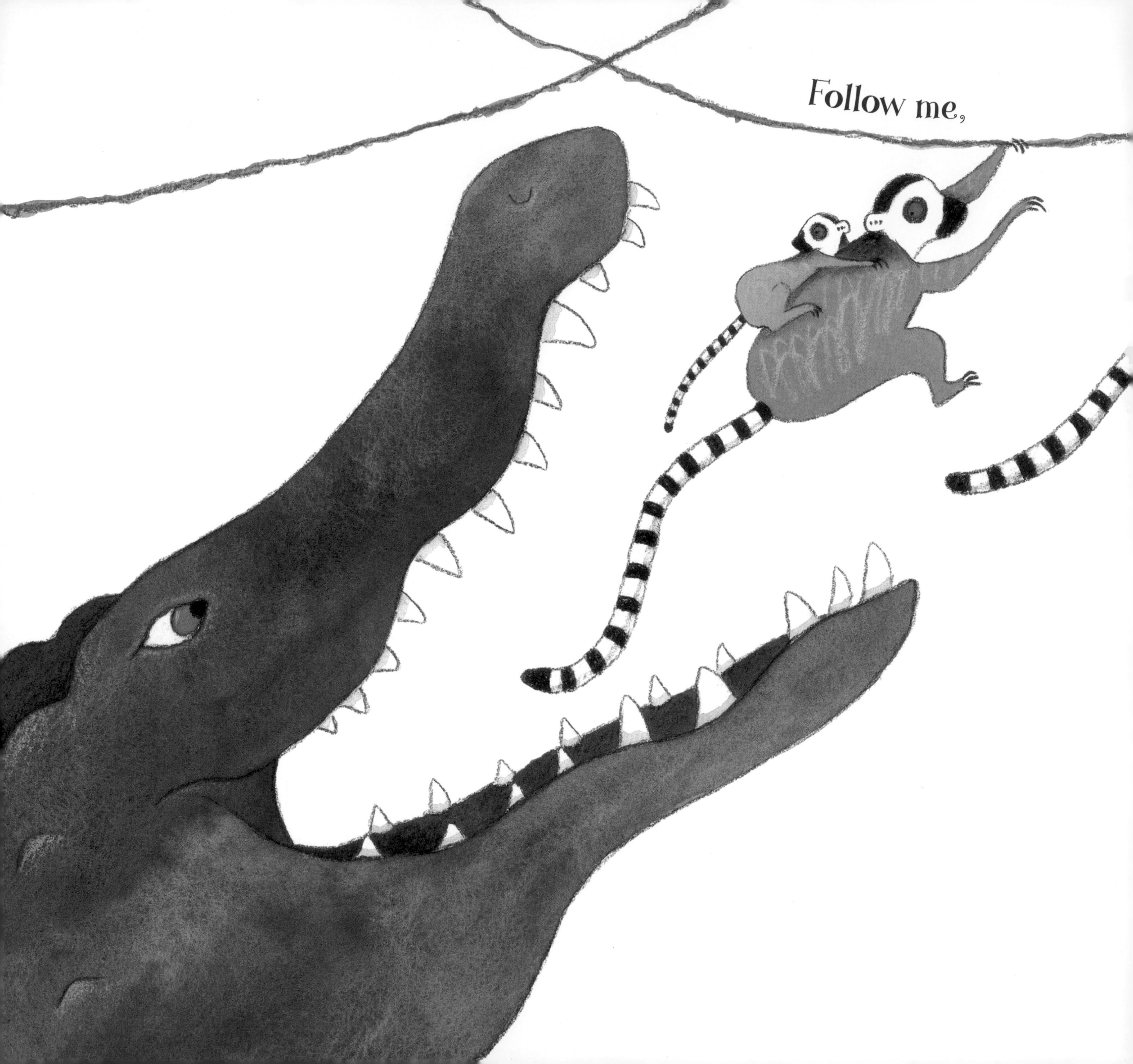

Follow me,

follow me,

follow me!

Phew!

Time to rest, come with me,

back we go to our tree.

Follow me...

follow me...

follow . . . zzzzzzzzzzzzzzzzzzzzzzz

Wait for me!

Look out for these great picture books,
perfect to share with children:
WHO puts the ANIMALS to BED?
MIJ KELLY and HOLLY CLIFTON-BROWN
YOU ARE (NOT) SMALL
by Anna Kang illustrated by Christopher Weyant
THAT RABBIT belongs to EMILY BROWN
CRESSIDA COWELL AND NEAL LAYTON
Please Mr Panda
Doughnuts
Steve Antony
OI FROG!
KES GRAY & JIM FIELD
For fun activities, further information and to order,
visit www.hodderchildrens.co.uk